U.S. Regions

The People of the Midwest

Blaine Wiseman

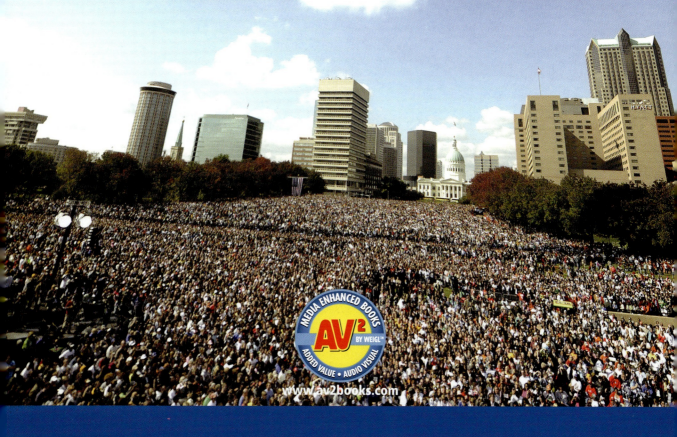

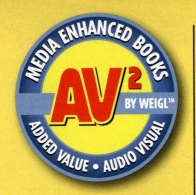

AV² provides enriched content that supplements and complements this book. Weigl's AV² books strive to create inspired learning and engage young minds in a total learning experience.

Your AV² Media Enhanced books come alive with...

 Audio
Listen to sections of the book read aloud.

 Key Words
Study vocabulary, and complete a matching word activity.

 Video
Watch informative video clips.

 Quizzes
Test your knowledge.

 Embedded Weblinks
Gain additional information for research.

 Slide Show
View images and captions, and prepare a presentation.

 Try This!
Complete activities and hands-on experiments.

... and much, much more!

Go to www.av2books.com, and enter this book's unique code.

BOOK CODE

N574209

AV² by Weigl brings you media enhanced books that support active learning.

Published by AV² by Weigl
350 5th Avenue, 59th Floor
New York, NY 10118

Websites: www.av2books.com   www.weigl.com

Copyright ©2015 AV² by Weigl
All rights reserved. No part of this publication may be reproduced, stored in a retrieval system, or transmitted in any form or by any means, electronic, mechanical, photocopying, recording, or otherwise, without the prior written permission of the publisher.

Library of Congress Control Number: 2014942116

ISBN 978-1-4896-2844-2 (hardcover)
ISBN 978-1-4896-2845-9 (softcover)
ISBN 978-1-4896-2846-6 (single-user eBook)
ISBN 978-1-4896-2847-3 (multi-user eBook)

Printed in the United States of America in North Mankato, Minnesota
1 2 3 4 5 6 7 8 9 18 17 16 15 14

062014
WEP060614

Project Coordinator: Aaron Carr
Designer: Mandy Christiansen

Every reasonable effort has been made to trace ownership and to obtain permission to reprint copyright material. The publishers would be pleased to have any errors or omissions brought to their attention so that they may be corrected in subsequent printings.

Weigl acknowledges Getty Images as its primary image supplier for this title.

Contents

AV² Book Code 2	Famous Midwesterners 20
Introducing the Midwest 4	Midwestern Politics 22
Settling the Midwest 6	Monuments and Buildings 24
Historic Events 8	Flags and Seals 26
Historic Midwesterners 10	Challenges Facing the Midwest 28
Cultural Groups 12	Quiz 30
Major Cities of the Midwest 14	Key Words/Index 31
Industries of the Midwest 16	Log on to www.av2books.com 32
Midwestern Tourism 18	

The People of the Midwest 3

Introducing the Midwest

The Midwest is a region transformed by the hard work of its people. Most of the grasslands that once covered the region have been turned into farmland. Vast prairies are dotted with cities and towns. From the Great Lakes to the shadow of the Rocky Mountains, millions of people have made their mark on the Midwest. They have built a region known for hard work, strong culture, and values.

Legend
- West (11 states)
- Southwest (5 states)
- Northeast (11 states)
- Southeast (11 states)
- Midwest (12 states)

Where People Live in the Midwest

Compare the populations of the biggest city in each Midwestern state.

City	Population
Fargo, **North Dakota**	109,779
Sioux Falls, **South Dakota**	159,908
Wichita, **Kansas**	385,577
Omaha, **Nebraska**	421,570

City	Population
Minneapolis, **Minnesota**	392,880
Des Moines, **Iowa**	206,688
Kansas City, **Missouri**	464,310
Chicago, **Illinois**	2,714,856

City	Population
Columbus, **Ohio**	809,798
Detroit, **Michigan**	701,475
Milwaukee, **Wisconsin**	598,916
Indianapolis, **Indiana**	834,852

*2012 population figures

The People of the Midwest 5

Settling the Midwest

Throughout its history, people have passed through the Midwest on their way somewhere else. Along the way, many have decided to stay and make it their home. The first people in the region were ancestors of American Indians. As the first North Americans spread out across the continent, rich cultures formed on the Great Plains.

European explorers traveled the region's rivers and set up trading posts. Still, most of the people in the region were American Indians from groups such as the Chippewa, Sioux, Fox, and many others. It all changed when the United States took over the Midwest. As the nation expanded, millions of people of European descent settled on the prairies. They began farming and built the region we know today.

★ Pioneers crossed the plains in large groups. They traveled in horse-drawn wagons.

Midwestern Migrations

700–1800s
By the 8th century, many different cultures had developed in the Midwest. **Mississippian cultures** built large pyramids and mounds out of earth, where they worshipped, celebrated, and worked together.

1700s–1800s
When Europeans began arriving in the Midwest, they were mostly fur traders. At first, they worked with the Mississippians, then French and English influences took over. The two nations fought over the land, bringing more people and war to the Midwest.

1825
When the Erie Canal was built, it opened the Midwest to settlers from the east. Stretching from the Hudson River to Lake Erie, it was the biggest construction project in U.S. history. Thousands of people migrated through the canal from New York to Ohio, Illinois, and Indiana.

1850s–1860s
The United States was expanding quickly, but travel was still slow. When railroad construction began, the Midwest became a very important region. By 1857, Chicago was the busiest railway city in the United States.

1862
During the **Civil War**, the U.S. government wanted to claim ownership of its territories. Through the Homestead Act, they gave land away for free. Millions of farmers, immigrants, and freed slaves moved west. They built homesteads on 80 million acres (32.4 million hectares) of prime farmland.

The People of the Midwest

Historic Events

The Midwest is located in the middle of North America. Many cultures and nations have tried to change and control the region. Whether they worked in cooperation or in conflict, these different groups of people have been important in the development of the Midwest. It is a region shaped by **monarchs**, politicians, warriors, and workers.

Pontiac's Rebellion (1763–1766)
Pontiac, a Shawnee American Indian leader, did not like the way his people were treated by the British and Americans. He brought together groups of the Great Lakes to fight back. Pontiac's Rebellion began at Detroit in 1763, and lasted until he was forced to surrender in 1766. Britain had defeated the French and the American Indians to take full control of the territory.

Louisiana Purchase (1803) The Louisiana Territory was a huge area of North America owned by France. It stretched from the Mississippi River to the Rocky Mountains and covered more than 800 million square miles (2 billion square kilometers). In 1803, the United States government bought the land for $15 million.

Lewis and Clark Expedition (1804–1806) Meriwether Lewis was hired to explore the Louisiana Territory. Lewis hired his friend, William Clark, to help. Lewis and Clark left Missouri in 1804 and spent two years exploring. They made many major discoveries throughout the Midwest and West, opening the land to other explorers and settlers.

Erie Canal (1825) In the early 19th century, the Appalachian Mountains made travel from the East to the Midwest difficult. The Erie Canal changed the route from a difficult mountain crossing to an easy float down the river. The canal created a water route between New York and Chicago.

Bleeding Kansas (1854–1859) While northern and southern states argued about slavery, there were no clear rules in U.S. territories. The Kansas-Nebraska Act left the decision of whether to allow slavery up to the people. Both sides rushed into Kansas, and violence broke out between them. Soon after, the Civil War began.

The Model T (1908) The Model T was not the world's first car, but it was the first car most people in the United States could afford. It was built in Detroit by Henry Ford, and by the 1920s, nearly half of the world's cars were Model Ts.

Historic Midwesterners

Many hard working, passionate, and innovative Midwesterners have had a major impact on history. They have changed their region, and some of them have changed the world. The most famous Midwesterners in history were explorers, inventors, fighters, and entertainers.

Mark Twain (1835–1910)
Samuel Langhorne Clemens was born and raised in Missouri, and grew up on the banks of the Mississippi River. He spent much of his life on the river. Clemens became famous as a writer under the name Mark Twain. With novels such as *The Adventures of Tom Sawyer* and *The Adventures of Huckleberry Finn*, Twain is often considered one of the greatest writers in the United States.

Sitting Bull (1831–1890)
When he was only 14 years old, Sitting Bull joined his first war party. When prospectors began arriving on land in what is now South Dakota, Sitting Bull fought back. He led many battles throughout his life, fighting for the rights of his people. His most famous fight was the Battle at Little Bighorn, where he led thousands of warriors against the U.S. Army.

Thomas Edison (1847–1931)
Thomas Alva Edison was born in Ohio and grew up in Port Huron, Michigan. Edison was homeschooled, and spent hours alone, reading, experimenting, and learning. He started his first business at 12 years old, and began inventing at 20. In his amazing life, Edison invented the automatic **telegraph** and the **phonograph**, and made improvements to the electric lightbulb.

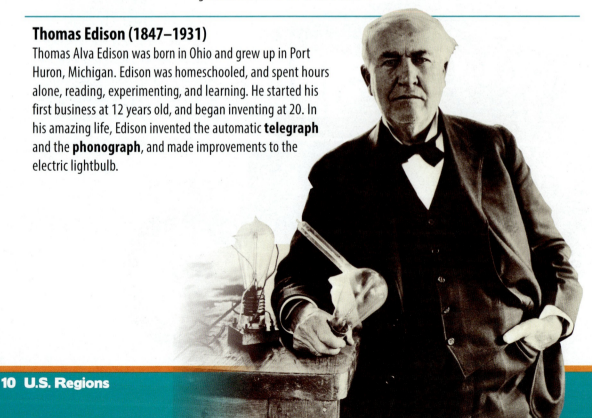

George Washington Carver (1864–1943)

Born into slavery in Diamond, Missouri, George Washington Carver became one of the best-known scientists in the United States. He became the first African American student at Iowa State University. Carver is known for his research into uses for the peanut. As well as food, he found it could be used for making shampoo, glue, gasoline, and other products.

Wilbur (1867–1912) and Orville Wright (1871–1948)

The Wright brothers grew up in Dayton, Ohio. In 1896, they began building their own design of the bicycle. This led to their next project. On December 17, 1903, they flew the world's first successful airplane.

Michael Jackson (1958–2009)

Michael Jackson was born in Gary, Indiana. When he was only 5 years old, he joined his older brothers in the group Jackson 5. Although the boys had many hit songs together, Michael began performing on his own at the age of 13. As a solo artist, he became known as "The King of Pop." His album, *Thriller*, is the best-selling album of all time.

Edison held 1,093 patents for inventions.

As a baby, Carver was **kidnapped** and **sold**, but was later found and returned to his home.

Cultural Groups

The Midwest has always been a region of strong communities. From the time of the Mississippian cultures to today, people have worked together to build the region. People of many different cultures have played a part in Midwestern history, and today there is wide diversity. Large African American, Asian, American Indian, and **Slavic** communities are common in the cities of the Midwest.

When the land of the Midwest was opened to homesteaders, Europeans of all backgrounds moved in. Farmers from Ireland, Germany, Sweden, Denmark, Ukraine, the Netherlands, and many other countries set up communities.

★ St. Patrick's Day is an Irish festival that is celebrated all over the world. In Ireland, it is a public holiday, and in other countries it is celebrated with dancing and parades.

Cultural Communities

While most Midwestern migrants adopted U.S. culture, others held onto their old traditions. Today, there are towns and communities reflecting this diverse history all over the region.

Bronzeville, Chicago, Illinois

In the 1920s, thousands of African Americans moved into the Chicago neighborhood of Bronzeville. They built a strong community that became known as the "Black Metropolis." Today, Bronzeville residents are trying to recapture the cultural identity of their neighborhood.

Frog Town, St. Paul, Minnesota

Frog Town gets its name from the swamp that used to cover the area. Today, it is known for its large population of **Hmong** people, and is part of St. Paul's "Little Mekong." Around 40 percent of the community's population is of Asian descent.

Elk Horn and Kimballton, Iowa

Two neighboring villages in Iowa are known as "Denmark on the Prairie." Danish immigrants began arriving in the mid-1800s. Today, Elk Horn and Kimballton are the largest rural Danish villages in the U.S. Elk Horn is home to the only working Danish windmill in the country.

New Ulm, Minnesota

New Ulm is named after the German city of Ulm. It was built in the 1850s by German settlers. Today, New Ulm's heritage is reflected in the sights and sounds of the city. A 45-foot (14 m) tall **glockenspiel** chimes throughout the day, and monuments show German legends.

The People of the Midwest

Major Cities of the Midwest

While the Midwest is known as a mostly rural region, it is also home to some of the biggest urban areas in the United States. The major cities of the region have played an important role in the country's history.

Located in the middle of Ohio, Columbus is the state capital and its largest city. The city's strong economy is led by the government, education, and insurance industries. Ohio State University is the largest college campus in the country.

More than 2 million people live in the Kansas City area, making it the biggest city in Missouri. It began as a trading post and grew when the railroad was built across the United States. The city's location, near the exact center of the U.S., makes it an excellent place to do business.

Indianapolis is a city known for its sports and education opportunities. The Indianapolis 500 and Brickyard 500 car races are the two biggest single-day sporting events in the world. These events create millions of dollars every year for the local economy. Many universities and colleges are located in the city, attracting thousands of students.

With almost 3 million residents, Chicago, Illinois, is the third largest city in the United States. It is known as "The Windy City" and is also a center of culture and history. It is one of the main transportation **hubs** in the country. The central location and access to other markets make Chicago a popular city for business.

In 1871, a fire broke out in Chicago, burning for more than two days as it spread from building to building. The Great Chicago Fire killed **more than 300 people** and left **100,000 homeless.**

The Children's Museum of Indianapolis is the largest children's museum in the world. It covers **472,900 square feet** (43,934 square meters). This is bigger than **eight football fields.**

State Capitals

State capitals are where politicians come together to make decisions that affect the entire state, region, and country. A state's capital is not always its biggest city, but it is always important. Some Midwestern capitals were chosen for their location or history, while others were chosen for the industries that drive them.

State Capitals	Population
Indianapolis, **Indiana**	834,852
Columbus, **Ohio**	809,798
St. Paul, **Minnesota**	290,770
Lincoln, **Nebraska**	265,404
Madison, **Wisconsin**	240,323
Des Moines, **Iowa**	206,688
Topeka, **Kansas**	127,939
Springfield, **Illinois**	117,126
Lansing, **Michigan**	113,996
Bismarck, **North Dakota**	64,751
Jefferson City, **Missouri**	43,183
Pierre, **South Dakota**	13,914

*2012 population figures

The People of the Midwest

Industries of the Midwest

The Midwest is often called "America's Breadbasket." This is because it is home to many of the country's top grain producers. The region also supports a strong **livestock** industry, while the oil and gas industries are growing. In Midwestern cities, manufacturing and services such as healthcare and finance are important businesses.

Iowa
Iowa is America's leading corn producer. Iowa's corn crop covers 13.7 million acres (5.5 million hectares), about twice the size of the entire state of Hawai'i.
- **2.2 billion bushels** of corn grown in 2013
- **$13.5 billion per year**

Michigan
Michigan is the home of the automotive industry and America's "Big Three." Ford, General Motors, and Chrysler all have their head offices in Michigan.
- **150,000 workers**
- Each year, the auto industry pays more than **$70 billion** in Michigan state taxes.

Nebraska
Nebraska is one of the leading agricultural states in the United States. There are 1.88 million beef cattle in Nebraska, and only about 1.86 million people.
- **20,000 beef cattle companies**
- **$12.1 billion per year**

North Dakota
North Dakota is America's second largest oil producer. There are almost 10,000 oil and gas wells in the state.
- 40,856 jobs
- $30.4 billion per year

South Dakota
Tourism is South Dakota's second-biggest industry. One in 11 South Dakotans work in tourism-related jobs.
- 27,958 jobs
- $1.98 billion per year

Minnesota
Minnesota is the second biggest producer of hogs in the United States. Farmers in Minnesota sell more than 15 million pigs every year.
- 3,355 hog farms
- $6.9 billion per year

Missouri
Manufacturing makes up a large part of Missouri's economy.
- 243,140 jobs
- $63 billion per year

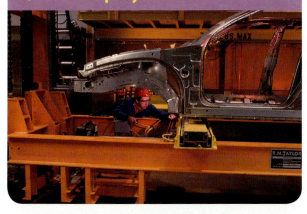

Kansas
Kansas is the number one wheat state in the country, producing 18 percent of U.S. wheat.
- 22,430 wheat farmers
- $3 billion per year

Ohio
Ohio is the 6th largest producer of soybeans in America. Soybeans are used for food, as well as for making plastics, fuels, and many other products.
- 26,000 soybean farmers
- $5.3 billion every year

Wisconsin
Wisconsin is known as "America's Dairyland." More than 13 percent of the country's milk and 25 percent of its cheese is produced in the state.
- More than 10,000 dairy farms
- $26.5 billion per year

The People of the Midwest

Midwestern Tourism

The most popular tourist attractions in the Midwest show just what makes the region unique. Millions of tourists are drawn every year to the region's historic, natural, and human-made attractions. From beautiful national parks to amazing feats of engineering, the Midwest has something for every tourist.

South Dakota
Carving started on Mount Rushmore in 1927. The faces of four presidents were carved by a sculptor named Gutzon Borglum. It took 14 years, and the help of about 350 people, to create the sculpture. Every year, more than 2.7 million people visit Mount Rushmore.

Nebraska
Omaha is home to both the world's largest indoor rainforest and desert. At Henry Doorly Zoo, visitors can explore these, along with Gorilla Valley, Bear Canyon, Orangutan Forest, and an aquarium. Each year, more than 1 million people visit the zoo.

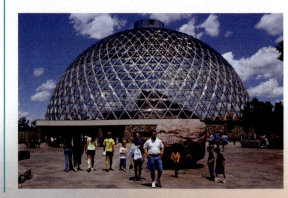

One of Theodore Roosevelt's favorite places in North Dakota was the Badlands. It is now a protected area called the Theodore Roosevelt National Park.

Iowa The Amana Colonies are a series of seven villages built by German settlers in the 1850s and 1860s. Everyone in the colonies worked together, sharing resources, land, and work. They lived this way until the Great Depression, in the 1930s. There are more than 800,000 visitors every year.

Illinois Navy Pier is located on Chicago's lakeshore. It covers 50 acres (20 hectares). During World War I and World War II, thousands of soldiers called the pier home. Today, it is home to the Chicago Children's Museum, a 15-story ferris wheel, parks, walkways, shops, and much more. Almost 9 million people visit Navy Pier every year.

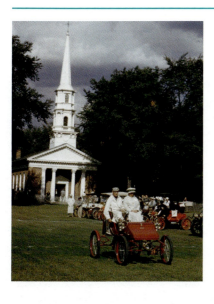

Michigan Henry Ford changed history with his innovations. He also started a collection of **artifacts** related to U.S. invention. Today, the collection in Detroit has grown to include 26 million items. The Henry Ford Museum attracts about 1.5 million visitors every year.

Missouri Towering over St. Louis, the Gateway Arch celebrates the expansion of the United States. The Jefferson National Expansion Memorial is a park that includes the 630-foot (192 meter) arch and the Western Expansion Museum. More than 2 million people visit each year, exploring the history of expansion, and riding a tram to the top of the arch.

Ohio Since 1892, people have been visiting Cedar Point, on the shores of Lake Erie, to ride roller coasters. Today, the Cedar Point Amusement Park is known as "The Roller Coaster Capital of the World." Each year, more than 3 million people visit Cedar Point to ride the 17 roller coasters in the park.

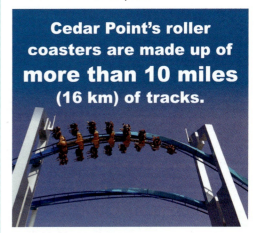

Cedar Point's roller coasters are made up of **more than 10 miles** (16 km) of tracks.

Indiana Indiana Dunes National Lakeshore runs for almost 25 miles (40 km) along Lake Michigan's southern shore. The area is home to diverse natural environments, including forests, wetlands, beaches, and sand dunes. About 2 million people visit the lakeshore every year.

The People of the Midwest

Famous Midwesterners

Midwesterners are known for their vision, hard work, and perseverance. When a Midwesterner needs something, they either go and get it, or go and build it. The most famous people from the region have built successful careers out of these Midwestern values.

Born in Cincinnati, Ohio, in 1946, **Steven Spielberg** has become one of the most successful directors in Hollywood. In 1975, Spielberg directed his first hit movie, *Jaws*. Since then he has made dozens of movies, such as *E.T. the Extra Terrestrial*, *Jurassic Park*, *The Color Purple*, and *Schindler's List*.

Madonna Ciccone was born in Bay City, Michigan, in 1968. Growing up, she was a passionate dancer with a unique style. In the 1980s, she became a pop music star with hits such as *Holiday* and *Like a Prayer*. Madonna has become the best selling female musician in the world.

Toni Morrison was born in Lorain, Ohio, in 1931. She loved reading and writing, which led to her career. In 1970, Morrison published her first novel, *The Bluest Eye*. In 1987, Morrison released *Beloved*, a book that became an instant classic, and won the Pulitzer Prize. Six years later, she became the first African American woman to win the Nobel Prize for literature.

Columbus, Ohio's **Jack Nicklaus** is often considered the greatest golfer of all time. "The Golden Bear" has won 18 major championships, more than any other golfer. For almost 30 years, Nicklaus dominated the Professional Golfer's Association (PGA). Nicklaus founded the Nicklaus Children's Health Care Foundation in 2004 to help sick children all over the country.

Warren Buffett was born in Omaha, Nebraska, in 1930. He was interested in finance, and was running his own business when he was just 13. He is known as "The Oracle of Omaha," for his ability to predict the stock market.

$$$ Warren Buffett has promised to donate his entire fortune, or $65 billion, to charity.

Quincy Jones was born in 1933. Jones has produced music for legends such as Frank Sinatra and Michael Jackson. He was also producer on three of Jackson's albums. Jones has been nominated for 79 Grammy awards, more than any other artist, and won 29.

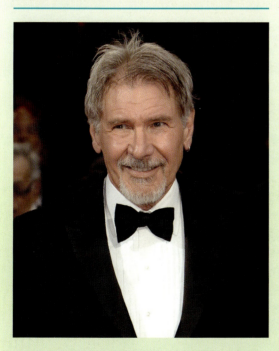

Chicago's **Harrison Ford** is one of Hollywood's best-known actors. Born in 1942, he struggled to find acting jobs before 1977. That year, his role as Han Solo in *Star Wars* made Ford a star. Other major roles include playing the heroes Indiana Jones and CIA agent Jack Ryan.

Lebron James became the youngest basketball player to reach 20,000 points, when he was only 28.

Lebron James was born in Akron, Ohio, in 1984. He achieved his dream of playing in the NBA when the nearby Cleveland Cavaliers drafted him in 2003. A basketball star growing up, James continued dominating as a professional. In 2010, he joined the Miami Heat and has led the team to two NBA Championships.

Midwestern Politics

A region of leaders, the Midwest plays a major role in the nation's politics. The Midwest has produced 11 U.S. presidents. These Midwestern presidents have led the nation through some of its most difficult periods.

Ohio's Ulysses S. Grant took over the presidency after the end of the Civil War. He was a hero during the war, leading Union troops to victory. Grant was president in charge during part of the Reconstruction era. He served two terms as president, from 1869 to 1877.

William Howard Taft was born in Cincinnati just before the Civil War. He wanted to be a Supreme Court Justice, but his wife and President Theodore Roosevelt wanted him to lead the Republican Party. Taft was president for one term, from 1909 to 1913, before returning to law. In 1921, he got the job he had always wanted—Chief Justice of the United States.

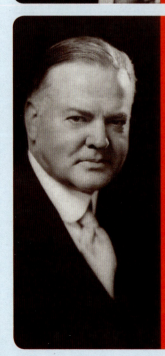

Herbert Hoover was born in Iowa in 1874. When he took over the presidency, the U.S. economy was as strong as it had ever been. Soon after, the markets crashed and the Great Depression began. He tried to end the Depression, but was voted out of the White House after only one term. One of Hoover's greatest achievements was building the Hoover Dam.

Harry S. Truman was born in Lamar, Missouri, and grew up outside Kansas City in the town of Independence. He became president near the end of World War II when President Franklin Roosevelt died. In 1945, he gave the orders for two atomic bombs to be dropped on the Japanese cities of Hiroshima and Nagasaki. Truman was re-elected and served until 1953.

State Politics

In the 2012 presidential election, six Midwestern states supported each of the major parties. Ohio, Iowa, and Wisconsin were **swing states** that helped the Democrats win the election.

Legend
(R)—Republican
(D)—Democratic

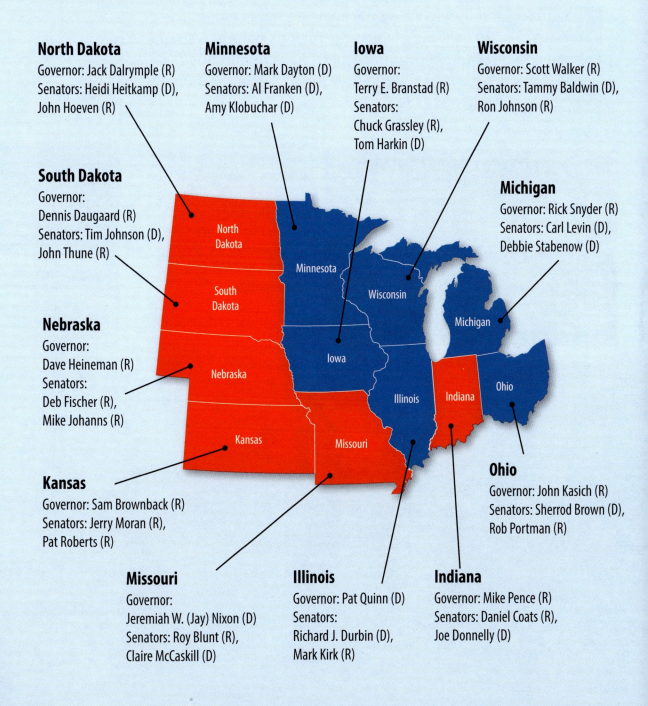

North Dakota
Governor: Jack Dalrymple (R)
Senators: Heidi Heitkamp (D), John Hoeven (R)

Minnesota
Governor: Mark Dayton (D)
Senators: Al Franken (D), Amy Klobuchar (D)

Iowa
Governor: Terry E. Branstad (R)
Senators: Chuck Grassley (R), Tom Harkin (D)

Wisconsin
Governor: Scott Walker (R)
Senators: Tammy Baldwin (D), Ron Johnson (R)

South Dakota
Governor: Dennis Daugaard (R)
Senators: Tim Johnson (D), John Thune (R)

Michigan
Governor: Rick Snyder (R)
Senators: Carl Levin (D), Debbie Stabenow (D)

Nebraska
Governor: Dave Heineman (R)
Senators: Deb Fischer (R), Mike Johanns (R)

Kansas
Governor: Sam Brownback (R)
Senators: Jerry Moran (R), Pat Roberts (R)

Ohio
Governor: John Kasich (R)
Senators: Sherrod Brown (D), Rob Portman (R)

Missouri
Governor: Jeremiah W. (Jay) Nixon (D)
Senators: Roy Blunt (R), Claire McCaskill (D)

Illinois
Governor: Pat Quinn (D)
Senators: Richard J. Durbin (D), Mark Kirk (R)

Indiana
Governor: Mike Pence (R)
Senators: Daniel Coats (R), Joe Donnelly (D)

The People of the Midwest 23

Monuments and Buildings

Engineers and builders have always been important to the Midwest. Throughout history, the region's natural resources have presented them with opportunities, barriers, and building materials. Midwesterners have helped build the United States and some of its biggest and most famous sites.

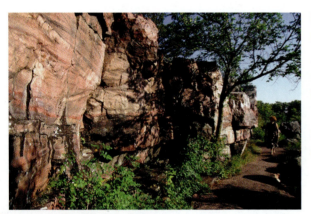

For 3,000 years, Pipestone National Monument in Minnesota has been an important site to American Indian cultures. The stone in the area is used to make ceremonial pipes. Today, people still use the pipestone, continuing valuable cultural traditions.

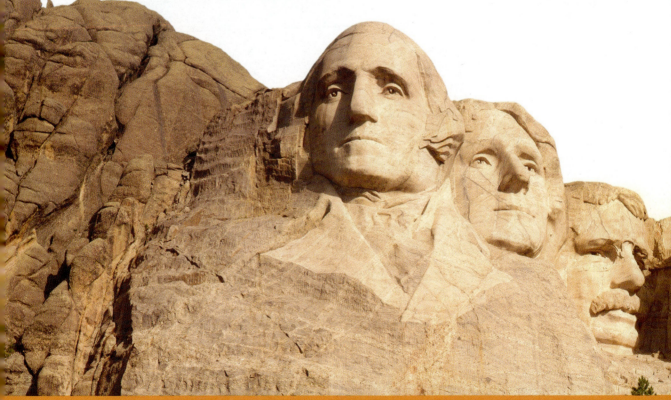

At 5 miles long, the Mackinac Bridge is one of the world's longest suspension bridges. The bridge opened in 1957, and cost more than $99 million to build. It stretches across the Straits of Mackinac, between Lake Michigan and Lake Huron, connecting the north and south parts of Michigan. Every month, around 200,000 cars cross the bridge.

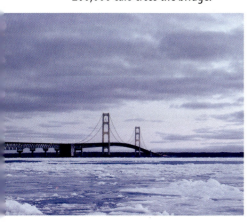

In 1973, a 110-story building opened in Chicago, becoming the tallest in the world. The 1,730-foot (527-m) Willis Tower was built over three years by 12,000 workers. It was the tallest building in the world until 1997. From the top floor, visitors get wide views of the Midwest. Illinois, Indiana, Michigan, and Wisconsin can all be seen from Willis Tower.

The Gateway Arch is a memorial to Thomas Jefferson and the pioneers who helped expand the nation. With the Louisiana Purchase of 1803, St. Louis became the gateway to the West. The Arch stands 630-feet (192-m) tall, and the base is 630 feet (192 m) long between the two legs. It opened in 1967 and cost more than $13 million to build.

South Dakota is home to Mount Rushmore. The faces of George Washington, Thomas Jefferson, Abraham Lincoln, and Theodore Roosevelt on Mount Rushmore are 60-feet (18 m) high.

The People of the Midwest 25

Flags and Seals

Flags and seals are used to show the symbols and values of a state. Flying over important buildings and sites, flags represent ownership. If multiple state flags are flown in the same place, they must be arranged properly. State flags are ordered by the date the state entered the Union.

Iowa

Flag The red, white, and blue bars stand for revolution and freedom. *Our Liberties We Prize and Our Rights We Will Maintain* is the state **motto**.

Seal The eagle is a symbol for the United States. The mountains represent the natural beauty of the state.

Ohio

Flag The swallowtail shape of the flag is based on the Ohio cavalry flag from the Civil War. The 13 stars on the left represent the original 13 states.

Seal The natural landscape is represented on the seal by the hills, fields, and water. The rays of the Sun show the 13 states, and the 17 arrows show that the 17th state is ready for war.

Minnesota

Flag The Minnesota flag features the state seal on a blue background. The 19 stars show Minnesota as being the 19th state to join the Union.

Seal The American Indian on horseback represents the American Indian heritage, and 1858 is the year Minnesota became a state.

Nebraska

Flag The flag is the state seal on a blue background.

Seal: The seal features the state motto, *Equality Before the Law*, and the date Nebraska became a state, March 1, 1867.

Wisconsin

Flag The Wisconsin flag is the state seal on a blue background, and 1848 is the year Wisconsin became a state.

Seal *Forward* is Wisconsin's state motto. Tools such as the plow, the pick and shovel, and the hammer stand for industry in the state.

Illinois

Flag Illinois' flag features the state seal on a white background.

Seal The eagle is a symbol for the United States. There are 13 stars and stripes, which stand for the original 13 colonies.

Kansas

Flag The Kansas flag features the state name and seal on a blue background, with a sunflower that stands for glory and light.

Seal *Ad Astra Per Aspera* ("To the Stars Through Adversity") is the state motto. Kansas was the 34th state so there are 34 stars on the seal.

Missouri

Flag Missouri's flag has red, white, and blue stripes and features its state seal.

Seal There are 24 stars on the state seal representing the 23 states in the Union before Missouri, with the large 24th star representing Missouri.

South Dakota

Flag South Dakota's seal is also on its flag. The flag has a pale blue background.

Seal 1889 is the year South Dakota became a state. The mountains represent the natural beauty and landscape of the state, and the farmer plowing his field shows its agriculture.

Michigan

Flag The flag shows the state seal on a field of blue.

Seal The eagle is a symbol for the United States, and the olive branch stands for peace.

North Dakota

Flag The eagle is a symbol for the United States. This flag features the motto of the United States, *E Pluribus Unum* ("Out of Many, One").

Seal October 1, 1889 is the date North Dakota adopted its state constitution, and "Liberty and Union Now and Forever One and Inseparable" is the state motto.

Indiana

Flag Indiana's torch stands for liberty and knowledge, and the rays of light represent the influence of liberty and knowledge.

Seal The woodsman with the ax shows the pioneer spirit of the state, and the sun rising behind the hills shows a bright future.

Challenges Facing the Midwest

Leaving It Behind

In the first half of the 20th century, the populations of many Midwestern cities grew. Booming automotive and manufacturing industries drew people from rural areas and other regions to the cities. Factories, malls, and entire neighborhoods sprang up. Cities such as Chicago, Detroit, and Cleveland were some of the wealthiest in the country.

Since the 1950s, jobs and people have been moving away from the Midwest. In 1970, more than 2 million people lived in Cleveland. Then, factories began closing down, moving to locations overseas. By 2010, there were less than 400,000 people left.

Detroit has been hit the hardest. Between 2000 and 2010, 25 percent of its population moved away. Many of its factories, malls, and neighborhoods are now abandoned. When the city could not pay back $20 billion in debt, Detroit went **bankrupt**.

Plowing It Up

Much of the Midwest is covered by grasslands. In the past, these prairie grasslands supported millions of buffalo and the American Indians who hunted them. When America expanded to include the Midwest, millions of people began farming in the region. Since then, they have been plowing native grasses and replacing them with crops.

★ The U.S. is ranked first in the world in corn production. Around 97 million acres (39 million ha) of land are used for corn.

These changes have been happening for more than a century, but have increased in recent years. Rising crop prices mean farmers are planting more crops. From 2006 to 2011, 1.3 million acres (526,000 ha) in the Dakotas, Nebraska, Iowa, and Minnesota were replaced by corn and soybeans. While rising prices are good news for farmers selling the crops, they are bad news for wildlife in the region. Grasslands provide food and shelter to important animal species such as honeybees, prairie dogs, and black-footed ferrets. When crops replace these habitats and food sources, the species leave the area or die off.

There are about 78,000 abandoned buildings in Detroit.

More than 70 percent of America's grasslands have been destroyed.

Quiz

1 What is the biggest city in the Midwest?

2 Which writer's real name was Samuel Langhorne Clemens?

3 Which state is called "The Crossroads of America?"

4 How many American presidents were born in the Midwest?

5 When did Europeans begin arriving in the Midwest?

6 Who is the Shawnee American Indian who led a rebellion?

7 Which European country's immigrants settled the towns of Elk Horn and Kimballton, Iowa?

8 How many Midwest state flags feature the state seal?

9 What is Missouri's biggest city?

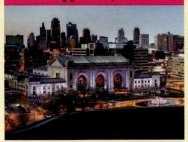

10 Which major Midwestern city went bankrupt?

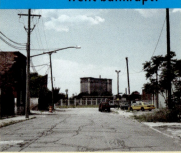

ANSWERS: 1. Chicago, Illinois 2. Mark Twain 3. Indiana 4. 11 5. 1700s–1800s 6. Pontiac 7. Denmark 8. Eight 9. Kansas City 10. Detroit, Michigan

30 U.S. Regions

Key Words

artifacts: items with historical or cultural meaning

bankrupt: unable to pay debts

Civil War: a war in the United States between the North and the South, 1861–1865

glockenspiel: a German musical clock

Hmong: a cultural group from mountain regions of China and Southeast Asia

hubs: centers of activities, regions, or networks

livestock: animals raised by humans for food

Mississippian cultures: mound-building Native American cultures that lived in the 700–1800s in parts of what is now the Midwestern, Eastern, and Southeastern U.S. These cultures grew crops such as corn, beans, and squash.

monarchs: rulers such as kings or queens who rule over a state or country, usually for life

motto: a short phrase that talks about values or beliefs

phonograph: a record player

Slavic: Eastern European

swing states: states in which there is no clear leading political party, and the win could go to any of the major parties

telegraph: a system that carries messages over a wire

Index

Chicago 4, 7, 9, 13, 14, 15, 19, 21, 25, 28
Cleveland 21, 28

Detroit 4, 8, 9, 14, 19, 28

Erie Canal 7, 9

Illinois 4, 7, 13, 15, 19, 23, 27
Indiana 4, 7, 11, 15, 16, 19, 21, 23, 25, 26
Iowa 4, 11, 13, 15, 16, 19, 22, 23, 26, 29

Kansas 4, 9, 15, 17, 23, 27
Kansas City 4, 14, 22

Michigan 4, 10, 15, 16, 19, 20, 23, 25, 27
Minnesota 4, 13, 15, 17, 23, 24, 26, 29
Missouri 4, 8, 10, 11, 14, 15, 17, 19, 22, 23, 27

Nebraska 4, 9, 15, 16, 18, 21, 23, 26, 29
North Dakota 4, 15, 17, 18, 23, 27, 29

Ohio 4, 7, 11, 14, 15, 17, 19, 20, 21, 22, 23, 26

South Dakota 4, 10, 15, 17, 18, 23, 25, 26, 27, 29
St. Louis 19, 25
St. Paul 13, 15

Wisconsin 4, 15, 17, 23, 25, 26

Log on to www.av2books.com

AV² by Weigl brings you media enhanced books that support active learning. Go to www.av2books.com, and enter the special code found on page 2 of this book. You will gain access to enriched and enhanced content that supplements and complements this book. Content includes video, audio, weblinks, quizzes, a slide show, and activities.

AV² Online Navigation

Book Pages
AV² pages directly correspond to pages in the book.

Key Words
Study vocabulary, and complete a matching word activity.

Quizzes
Test your knowledge.

Slide Show
View images and captions, and prepare a presentation.

Audio
Listen to sections of the book read aloud.

Video
Watch informative video clips.

Embedded Weblinks
Gain additional information for research.

Try This!
Complete activities and hands-on experiments.

AV² was built to bridge the gap between print and digital. We encourage you to tell us what you like and what you want to see in the future.

Sign up to be an AV² Ambassador at www.av2books.com/ambassador.

Due to the dynamic nature of the Internet, some of the URLs and activities provided as part of AV² by Weigl may have changed or ceased to exist. AV² by Weigl accepts no responsibility for any such changes. All media enhanced books are regularly monitored to update addresses and sites in a timely manner. Contact AV² by Weigl at 1-866-649-3445 or av2books@weigl.com with any questions, comments, or feedback.